SWORDFISH RETURNS

SMITHSONIAN OCEANIC COLLECTION

For my parents, who have always loved the sea — S.K.

For all The Family — D.J.S.

Book copyright © Trudy Corporation and the Smithsonian Institution, Washington DC 20560

Published by Soundprints Division of Trudy Corporation, Norwalk, Connecticut

Book design: Shields & Partners, Westport, CT
Book layout: Marcin D. Pilchowski, Jennifer Kinon
Editor: Laura Gates Galvin
Editorial assistance: Chelsea Shriver

First Edition 2003
10 9 8 7 6 5 4 3 2 1
Printed in China

Acknowledgments:
    Our very special thanks to Dr. Stanley H. Weitzman of the National Museum of Natural History's Department of Vertebrate Zoology for his curatorial review.
    Soundprints would like to thank Ellen Nanney and Robyn Bissette at the Smithsonian Institution's Office of Product Development and Licensing for her help in the creation of this book.

SWORDFISH RETURNS

by Susan Korman   Illustrated by Daniel J. Stegos

Soundprints
Where Children Discover...

It is late February when a mother swordfish reaches the warm waters of the Caribbean Sea. She has traveled here from the North Atlantic Ocean to lay her eggs.

The mother swordfish releases millions of eggs into the sea. Her mate fertilizes the eggs, as she swims away. Her time as a mother is done, even before the baby fish hatch.

The tiny eggs float in the water. Hungry fish eat many of them. Nearly three days pass before the surviving eggs hatch.

When Baby Swordfish finally hatches, he does not look at all like his mother! He is covered with scales, which have small spines. His fins are not fully formed yet and his upper and lower jaws are lined with sharp teeth. But soon all this will change.

Baby Swordfish feeds in deep waters. At first he eats mostly the eggs or young of other fish. As he grows, he begins feeding on other, bigger things—small fish, squid, crabs, lobsters, and clams.

Swordfish's body changes as the months pass. His dorsal fin now stands high behind his head like a sail. His upper jaw grows longer than his lower jaw. This gives him a bill that looks like a sword.

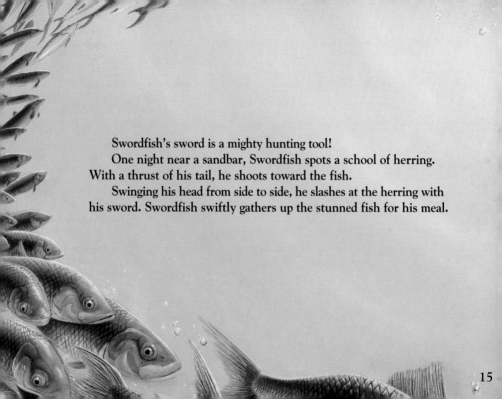

Swordfish's sword is a mighty hunting tool!

One night near a sandbar, Swordfish spots a school of herring. With a thrust of his tail, he shoots toward the fish.

Swinging his head from side to side, he slashes at the herring with his sword. Swordfish swiftly gathers up the stunned fish for his meal.

16

Swordfish feeds often. By now he has lost all his teeth, and he can swallow his prey without chewing!

One night, while he is feeding, Swordfish senses danger. A large, dark form draws closer—it is a mako shark!

The mako shark is large—and a very fast swimmer.
But Swordfish can swim fast, too. His strong tail muscles give him power. His long, streamlined body and tail fin give him speed.

The hungry shark chases Swordfish through the water. Swordfish races away frantically. The mako has almost caught up when a bluefish flutters past.

21

The mako suddenly spots the bluefish. The bluefish is easier prey. The mako turns from Swordfish and dips toward the bluefish. For now, Swordfish is safe.

As summer approaches, Swordfish begins his long journey north to the Atlantic Ocean. Sometimes he swims near the surface. When the water is calm, he leaps upward, his sleek, blue back and tall dorsal fin flashing brightly above the water.

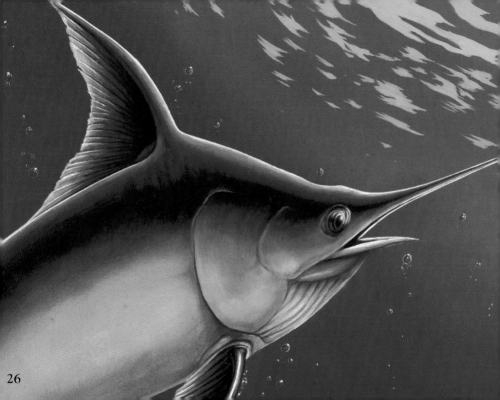

One morning near dawn, Swordfish swims up toward the surface in search of food. Suddenly, something unusual catches his eye.

Swordfish slowly swims toward the strange glow. A long line, baited with squid and mackerel, hangs in the water. Several other swordfish and marlin swim nearby.

Swordfish draws nearer. But then something unexpected happens. Abruptly, the line is yanked from the water, and the food is gone.

Startled, Swordfish swims away. He will search for food somewhere else.

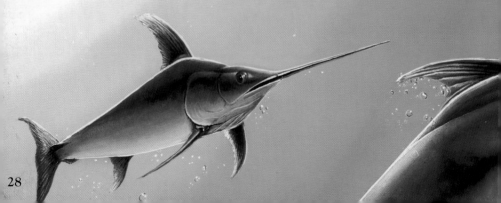

A few months pass and Swordfish reaches the Atlantic Ocean. But as winter approaches, Swordfish begins another journey. This time, he heads south, toward the warmer waters where he himself was hatched.

About the North Atlantic Swordfish

The swordfish ranges throughout all the oceans of the world, as well as the Black and Mediterranean Seas. It lives in temperate and tropical waters, and occasionally in cold waters. It is often grouped with the sailfish and marlin as a type of billfish, but actually belongs to a different family of fishes.

As its name implies, the bill, or "sword," of a swordfish is its most distinctive feature. The swordfish uses this bony projection of its upper jaw to strike smaller fish for food. However, it is also believed that the swordfish uses this bill to cut water as it swims, enhancing its speed and making the swordfish one of the fastest fish in the sea. It can swim up to 60 miles per hour! The swordfish's sword can grow up to four or five feet long, often about one-third of the fish's total length. Female swordfish may grow as long as 14 feet and weigh up to 1,200 pounds, while male swordfish grow to an average length of six to ten feet and weigh between 130 and 265 pounds.

Because of its unusual beauty, the swordfish is a prized game fish. Commercial fishermen usually use long lines to capture swordfish, using squid, mackerel and light sticks as bait. Due to overfishing, the swordfish population has declined in recent years, requiring government restrictions upon fishing at times.

Glossary

dorsal fin: A fin that grows along a fish's back, which helps to keep the fish upright.
prey: An animal that is hunted as food.
spine: A pointed bump on a fish's scale.
bill: A beaklike mouthpart.
mackerel: Very small, fatty Atlantic fish.